With love,

MW01114583

Buddy is Sandy's father. Buddy is a Golden Retriever. Sandy is Buddy's daughter. Sandy is a Golden Doodle.

A Golden Doodle has a father that is a Golden Retriever, and a mother that is a Poodle.

Sandy is Teddy's sister, and Teddy is Sandy's brother.

Sandy is standing up, and Teddy is laying down.

Teddy is bigger than Sandy.

Sandy loves to watch the different colored fish swimming in the fish tank.

The children and their parents enjoy looking at the different fish in the big fish tank. There are small fish, and bigger fish. There are different colored fish.

Some fish are red, some are blue, some are orange, some are yellow, some are green, some have more than one color. One fish is blue and black with yellow tail fins.

"Sandy be careful, please don't touch the fish tank!"

"Sandy, move away from the fish tank. Sandy don't bump into the fish tank!"

Do you know what happened?

Sandy was so close, she bumped into the fish tank.

When Sandy bumped into the fish tank, a small orange fish flew out of the water, then it fell back into the water!

Sandy was so close to the fish tank that she bumped into it again! Water splashed over the top, and a fish fell onto Sandy's head!

"What is going on here?" asked the children's mother. "Sandy, how did that fish get on your head?"

When the children's father saw this he gently picked up the fish and put it back into the fish tank.

Can you name the colors of the fish on Sandy's head?

This is Sandy and Daisy.

Daisy is Sandy's aunt. When Daisy visits Sandy, they like to play in the backyard together. When they see or hear someone walking near their home they bark loudly:

Ruff! Ruff! Ruff! ARFF! ARFF! ARFF!!

If they see someone walking their dog they bark RUFF! RUFF! RUFF!

If they hear someone delivering the mail they bark: RUFF! RUFF! RUFF!

Sometimes when one dog starts barking, all the other dogs start barking! RUFF!

RUFF! RUFF!! RUFF!!

It can get very loud!

Schultz is the biggest dog in Sandy's family!

Schultz and Sandy are cousins.

When Schultz visits Sandy, they like to play together.

If they see a rabbit, they will both bark at it: Arf! Arf! Arf!! Ruff!, Ruff!, Ruff!!

The children's father says, "Ok Sandy, let's play Roll Over." First, Sandy lays down on the floor. Then the children's father pushes on Sandy's chest, and rolls her over on her side. Then he says, "Roll Over", and rolls her over on her other side. The children's father keeps rolling Sandy over as he says, "Roll Over, Roll Back, Roll Over, Roll Back, Roll Over, Roll Back, Roll Over, Roll Back"

Do you think Sandy likes this game?

Bootsy is Sandy's cousin. When the children's father opens the back door, Bootsy and Sandy like to run together in the back yard. They bark at the animals and birds they see.

Can you name these dogs?

If you said Sandy, and her brother Teddy, you are right!

This is Buddy, Lucy, and Sandy. Buddy is Sandy's father, and Lucy is Sandy's mother.

They like it when children talk to them and pet them.

Sandy was born in the month of November, just before Thanksgiving. Thanksgiving is a holiday when we thank God for all the good things He gives us to enjoy. We enjoy our families, our friends, and our pets,

Can you name all the people in your family?

Do you have a pet in your family?

The family decided to have a birthday party for Sandy in November. The children's father and mother said they could invite their friends. Everyone sang: "Happy birthday to you, happy birthday to you, happy birthday dear Sandy, happy birthday to you!"

When Sandy heard the children singing, she tried singing too. Dogs can't sing, but they can bark. When Sandy started to sing, she barked: ARF ARF ARF ARF ARF ARF. RUFF, RUFF, RUFF, RUFF, RUFF, RUFF.

"Sandy, don't touch the cupcakes, they are for the children!" The children's mother gave Sandy a cracker to eat.

Can you guess how old Sandy is?

Sandy walked away from the table where the children were eating cupcakes.

Can you guess what Sandy went to look at?

"Sandy, Please Don't Touch The Fish Tank With Your Nose!!"

Can you name all the dogs in Sandy's family?
Can you point to each dog and say their name?

Sandy is tired.

SHHHHH Its time to go to sleep.

Goodnight Sandy,

We Love You!

Sandy Loves You, Too!

Printed in the USA
CPSIA information can be obtained
at www.ICGtesting.com
LVHW070809210824
788810LV00001B/1